C000100001

To my children Max, Julia and Maria.

To my granddaughter Astrid.

To my "adopted" son Russell.

THE ADVENTURES OF CALIGULA,

A SPHYNX CAT

BY

ANNA GREAVES

Chapter 1

MY BIRTH IN BONNY SCOTLAND

Hi, everyone! My name is Caligula. I'm an unusual, intelligent and affectionate type of cat, who loves people. I'm going to tell you my life story so far, and why and how I moved, from my native land, to another country across the border. I was born on a cold but sunny day in April, on a farm north of Edinburgh, in beautiful Scotland. Spring was in the air and the birds were singing in the apple orchard at the back of the farm. All the fruit trees were covered in clouds of blossom, either pink or white. Clusters of yellow daffodils and red tulips dotted the green lawns around the main house, an old white cottage with a thatched roof.

This was the home of my masters, the Macmillan family. My parents, two sphynx cats, were the Macmillan's family pets, but any kittens born from them were sold on, as we are a rare breed and some people are prepared to pay good money for us.

I remember well the room where I was born. There was a huge fireplace, with a red rug in front of it. A low, pine coffee table stood there, with two green sofas flanking each side. A cluttered sideboard stood by the fireplace. Lots of pictures showing sphynx cats hung on one of the walls. I discovered later that they were portraits of my ancestors. A coarse, musical noise drifted into the room from elsewhere in the house. I later learnt that this was the sound of Mr. Macmillan's bagpipes

When I opened my eyes for the first time, I saw my father, Bertie. He appeared very regal, curled up on the rug by the roaring fire. Purring loudly, it was clear that he was delighted to be a dad again. His body was mostly grey, with a few white markings on his chest and more above his nose. The skin on his forehead and the back of his neck bore deep folds, and he had very large ears indeed.

Next to him was my mother, Poppy. She was quite pink, also sporting big ears and wrinkles. She was very beautiful and instantly I felt that I loved her. Then

I spotted a small pink bundle close to my mother: it was my sister. I was so happy to belong to such a wonderful family!

However, I remember feeling quite cold soon after I was born, in spite of the rug. After being so warm in my mother's tummy, I started to realize that the world was a chilly place. Despite the log fire crackling in the fireplace, I was shivering so much that my teeth chattered non-stop, so I snuggled closer to my sister. Luckily for us, we had warm milk on tap! Staying close to Mum made me feel so secure, warm and contented.

After a big helping of Mum's milk, I decided to take a closer look at those pictures on the wall. The cats shown *were* like Mum and Dad. However, I also noticed pictures of cats covered in fur of different colours on one of the back walls of the lounge. Looking again at Dad, I noticed that he seemed to be completely *without* fur, except for some fine grey down on his tail. I then checked Mum; she too seemed to be furless, just like him.

"So," I said to myself, "if Mum, Dad *and* my sister have no fur, then *I* probably have no fur. And *that's* why I feel so cold!" Glancing down at my limbs and tail, I could see that they were grey like my father's, but I too had NO FUR! Just the thought of being bald made me shiver even more. I snuggled even closer to Mum.

"Mummy, why do some of the cats in those pictures have fur, when we don't?" I asked Mum.

"Dear son," she replied, "we're different from them. We're a *special* breed of cat, called Sphynx. Our oldest ancestor was Elizabeth, a barn cat who lived in Ontario, Canada, a long time ago. One of Elizabeth's kittens was born with no fur in 1966. It was just one of those things that happen by chance. Then she added "There are actually only about two thousand of us in the world. You should be proud to be a sphynx; we're very unique, you know...".

I felt very special when I heard that, - especially as Mum said that I looked very much like my Dad.

"Are furry cats anything like us, Mum? Or do they behave differently?" I asked, fascinated.

"I believe that they're more or less the same, son. Personally, I have never met one. I always wondered whether they like the same things we do, though; for example, do they like tuna fish as much as your father and I do? I wonder. Maybe you will get to ask one, someday," she replied. I wondered how I might ever meet a cat with fur! Maybe the Macmillans would get one? I suppose they must have owned furry cats in the past, judging by the pictures on the back wall of the lounge.

Our peace and quiet did not last long, as at that very moment, the door opened. Mr. and Mrs. Macmillan entered to marvel at us. Mrs. Macmillan was a red-haired woman in her thirties, with very round eyes that gave her a permanent look of surprise. Her husband was a tall, dark-haired man, dressed in a kilt - the family tartan, complete with sporran - about ten years older than his wife. A bushy moustache rested under his large, reddish nose. A pair of twinkly brown eyes gave him a kind, affable look, and his rosy cheeks betrayed the fact that he enjoyed the odd snifter of Scotch whisky.

"Look how cute the kittens are!" exclaimed Mrs. Macmillan, her eyes becoming wider and rounder than before. Mr. Macmillan agreed wholeheartedly.

"Gorgeous they certainly are, my dear," he said. "I especially like the grey one."

His eyes sparkled as he peered down at us. Mrs. Macmillan continued to examine us with great interest and added,

"You know, I think the grey one is male and the pink one is female. We've got a boy and a girl!".

And at that point, their children rushed in: a boy, Duncan, and his younger sister, Aila. Duncan was 12 years old, with a head of unruly dark hair that kept falling over his eyes. His face was perfectly round like a porcelain dish. He had a very eager look in his eye. Aila was 10 years old, with mousy-coloured hair. The girl was gentle and quiet; I liked her. But it was Duncan who lunged towards me, grabbing me roughly and shouting excitedly,

"This one is mine! I'll call him Caligula, after one of the Roman emperors I'm studying at school!" Then Aila approached. She gently picked my sister up and declared,

"This kitten shall be mine, then. I'll call her Coira, like my best friend."

I didn't like Duncan too much at first, as it did hurt when he grabbed me. I was also terrified that I would be dropped; Duncan was a clumsy boy who did not even bother to tie his shoelaces at times. My parents looked on, worried too. I held on to Duncan's arm for dear life. Duncan shouted,

"Ouch, Caligula, you scratched my arm. Naughty cat. *Naughty*!" Thankfully, at that point, he laid me back down next to my mother.

"What a lucky escape," I thought, getting my breath back.

Chapter 2

MY HAPPY KITTENHOOD

As the days went by, and then the weeks, my sister and I grew stronger and the weather became warmer. We soon started to eat solid food, and we especially liked tuna fish and crunchy cat biscuits. We loved being kittens, as we had a good excuse for being constantly mischievous.

Coira and I would chase each other constantly and often engaged in games of rough-and-tumble all over the house. We would run up and down the staircase many times every day and also used to grip our way up curtains and furniture, as fast as we could, as if we were having some sort of race. I usually managed to climb up first, for I seemed to be a little stronger than Coira.

Our favourite room was the enormous kitchen with an ancient cooker, called an Aga, along one of the walls, and a massive rectangular table in the middle. Coira and I would run round and round the table, until we felt dizzy and had to stop.

When Duncan came back from school, I would slip quietly behind the cluttered sideboard in the room where I was born. However, Duncan soon learnt that, if he shut the door of this room, I could no longer hide away from him. When he picked me up, he would sit me on his lap and stroked me for a long time. I hated it; Duncan's hands were *always* cold. I would end up shivering and shaking like a leaf. I always suspected that he liked to warm his hands on my body, especially as we, sphynx cats, have a very warm and soft skin, which feels like chamois leather.

Sometimes, when he played with us, I liked Duncan a little. He would often wave some sort of fishing rod that had a squeaky toy mouse at the end. Coira and I enjoyed jumping up and trying to catch it.

At first, the Macmillans did not allow me and Coira out of the house; they thought we might get lost and, in any case, it was far too cold for us. However, after a few weeks, when Coira and I were older and the weather was much warmer, they started leaving the front door open. It was an exciting thought: we could now follow our parents into that big, wide and scary world outside.

The first time, we went out timidly, watching the strange creatures on the branches of the yew tree at the front of the house. These creatures made chirping noises. Oddly, I felt a great urge to climb up the trees and try to catch one, just as I did with Duncan's squeaky toy mouse. It was much more difficult however, as these creatures could fly.

Coira and I would make a funny noise when we saw the creatures. We called this noise "clacking". We would move our lower jaw up and down very quickly and sometimes we would accompany this with a wobbly 'meow'. We couldn't help it any more than if our teeth were chattering in the cold. Mum and Dad told us that this was something all cats do when they see prey.

"Those creatures in the trees are called *birds*," said Dad. "They come in different sizes. Some birds are huge, such as *swans*. I would leave swans well alone; they can be vicious creatures. But there are smaller birds, like those in the tree. They're prey - and they do taste very good indeed - but you're too young to get up there just yet. In any case, humans are fond of birds, and they don't want us to catch any."

As I was quite stubborn, however, I decided to try my luck one day, when my parents were asleep in a sunny spot at the back of the house and, for once, were not keeping an eye on me. I sneaked away quietly, followed by Coira, and saw a bird landing on the higher branches of the larger yew tree. I ran up the tree as fast as I could - not a difficult thing to do, if you're careful to sharpen your claws - but sadly my efforts were wasted. The bird flew away before I could even reach it. I needed to be *much* faster.

Up there in the branches, an awful thought occurred to me. Getting up the tree was one thing, but getting down was quite another. I was stuck! I mewed so loudly in distress, that not only my parents, but also Mr. Macmillan came to my rescue. He had to climb on a ladder, as he couldn't reach me from the ground. Eventually, I was safe in his arms.

"There you are, Caligula! You really are a silly kitten, trying to climb up such tall trees," said my master. "Make sure you don't do this again," he added briskly, giving me a friendly wink. My parents were relieved that I had not done myself an injury. I did, however, receive a good telling-off for my foolishness, although they both hugged me tightly afterwards, making it clear that they were glad I was safe.

I resigned myself to leaving birds alone in future and, spurred on by my parents, I enjoyed chasing mice instead. Dad told me that our masters would be very pleased if we caught a mouse or two. It wasn't good for the Macmillans if there were mice in their kitchen. Mice would munch their way through cereal packets and cause all manner of mess there, as well as being a health hazard, with their horrible droppings left everywhere they went.

I remember, one day, coming face to face with one of these creatures. The second I entered the kitchen that night, I could smell something strange. I saw something darting quickly across the floor, towards the refrigerator, then disappearing beneath it. Peering under, I caught a glimpse of a tiny brown body with a glinting pair of black, beady eyes. The mouse was just a few inches back and a feeling of excitement seized me.

My instinct told me that I had to pounce on it and sink my teeth into its neck. But it was no use; this mouse was not coming out as long as I was waiting there.

Fortunately, Dad came to my rescue, as I lacked experience and did not know what to do next. In one deft movement, Dad swept his long paw under the refrigerator, produced the mouse, and delivered it into his mouth before the creature even knew what had happened. Whilst I hurried along behind him in admiration, Dad rushed the mouse to Mrs. Macmillan, to lay it at her feet. She was very pleased with my father.

"Good boy, Bertie!" she beamed. "Carry on catching these horrible little pests!" You see, Mrs. Macmillan was terrified of mice and always climbed on the nearest piece of furniture, screaming shrilly whenever she saw a live mouse. She immediately rewarded Dad with a few pieces of the juiciest roast chicken, which he was happy to share with the rest of us.

Chapter 3

MY JOURNEY SOUTH

When I turned ten weeks old, I began to notice that my parents were looking increasingly subdued. They were simply not their usual selves. Dad never seemed to be in the mood for stalking mice in the kitchen; instead, I would often catch him looking at me wistfully. Mum too seemed very distant and had trouble sleeping. Such an unsettling atmosphere left Coira and me feeling very distressed.

One day, determined to discover the cause of the mournful mood, I confronted my parents. "There's something wrong, isn't there? Why are you both behaving so strangely?" Coira stood at my side. Mum shot a meaningful sidelong glance at Dad. Dad nodded. "It's time," he said solemnly. Then Mum spoke:

"Caligula, Coira. You're getting big now. You're almost twelve weeks old. An unhappy time is approaching, for all of us - " She broke off and looked at the floor.

"What is it, Mum? What's going to happen?" Coira demanded, clearly upset. Dad interjected, speaking slowly.

"A time comes in every sphynx's life when it's time to leave. You must soon leave us - and the Macmillans. A stunned silence followed. Dad continued,

"Both your mother and I left our families when we were roughly your age. We have brothers, sisters and parents somewhere. We even have sons and daughters, probably all over the country and beyond."

Actually, my parents had lost count of how many of their offspring the Macmillans had already sold. They thought that perhaps they were about nine, but could not remember exactly. I had no clue about any of this, and therefore I had lived a carefree, happy life. Until now, that is.

"This morning," Dad added, "I heard Duncan saying to his friend that an English family has already paid a thousand pounds for you, Caligula!" There was a flash of pride in his eyes as he spoke. A thousand pounds! That sounded an enormous sum of money!

I was flattered and astonished by the fact that I was worth so much, but immediately afterwards, I was hit by extreme sadness. The thought of having to leave my parents, my sister, my comfortable home, my beautiful Scotland - was truly horrifying. I was afraid of the future. I did not know whether I would see my parents and Coira ever again!

"Now listen to me, Caligula," said Mum, with a note of gravity in her voice. "We do not know exactly when you will be moved. But whenever and wherever you go, remember always to be polite to everybody you meet. Purring will show others that you are good-mannered and friendly, so remember to purr, if you want to be liked. And remember to wash behind your ears."

That dreaded day came soon enough. Early one morning, Mrs. Macmillan came to find me. I was dozing happily on the red rug in the lounge, feeling as contented as the day I was born. A steady, slightly discordant drone sounded in my dream as Mr. Macmillan piped his favourite tune, 'Brave Scotland'. Mrs. Macmillan bent down and gently picked me up, waking me from my warm sleep with a start. She cradled me in her arms.

"Come on, Caligula," she said in her softest voice, "your big day has arrived. You're going on an airplane today!" A sinking feeling hit me hard in the stomach. What about my family?

Mrs. Macmillan put me in a white plastic cat carrier and shut me in. I tried to scratch the door and the sides of the carrier. I wanted to escape, to find my parents and Coira. I tried and tried, but I could not get out of that plastic cage! My claws hurt from my struggle with the door. I had no choice but sit down, resigned to my fate, on the yellow blanket that my mistress had folded neatly and placed in the carrier. This was it. I didn't even get to say goodbye.

Mrs. Macmillan heaved me into the boot of her car. She called out to her husband that she was ready to leave for the airport. Mr. Macmillan rushed out of the house and yelled,

" Okay, dear! Drive carefully. It's a good thing Duncan and Aila are at school today, or they would be very upset. Good bye, Caligula. I hope you'll like your new home!"

With all sense of hope disappearing fast, I mewed and mewed, as loudly as I possibly could, for my parents and my sister to come out to say goodbye. But they couldn't. The front door was shut.

The journey to the airport was terrible. It was bumpy and dark in the boot of the car. I missed my family more than I could bear. I didn't want to go to another family in England. I wanted to stay with my parents, with Coira, with the Macmillans!

At the airport, a young lady in a blue and red uniform - an air stewardess - took me across the tarmac to a gigantic airplane. I had seen airplanes high in the sky many times before, but they seemed to be just tiny dots. I assumed that they must be much the same as birds. But this one was a *monster* and so much bigger than me!

The stewardess handed me to a man in blue overalls. I didn't know who he was either, or what he wanted with me. I was still trapped in my white cage, trying to claw my way out again. The man took me through a vast opening, into the hold of the airplane, where lots of bags and suitcases had already been piled high. He tied my carrier, with thick nylon black ropes, to a large metal ring attached to the body of the plane. Nobody would hear my cries in here!

I noticed that, close by, there was another carrier, also tied to a metal ring. A grey and white cat was inside the carrier, sprawled comfortably on a purple blanket. She spoke cheerily to me, telling me her name was Sophie.

Sophie had fur! She said that her masters too were travelling on the plane and were going to London to visit relatives. They would be returning home after two weeks. This was the fifth time she was flying, she told me with a touch of pride, and she was used to it.

I was far too cold and terrified to speak. I couldn't even manage a purr. I wanted to ask her if she liked eating tuna fish, but the words just wouldn't come. I succeeded in getting under the yellow blanket Mrs. Macmillan had used to line the base of the carrier. After a while, in spite of the noise made by the engines, I fell asleep, exhausted. I didn't even notice the lift-off.

The next thing I was aware of, was violent shaking. I jumped up, alarmed, but I was thrown against the side of the carrier. Again, I started to mew loudly. I heard Sophie's voice trying to reassure me,

"Hey, don't be afraid. We're only going through a storm. The safest thing is for you to lie down, while it lasts." Her voice was serene and reassuring. I remembered that Mum was miles away and missed her dreadfully.

Thankfully, the plane stopped shuddering soon afterwards and the rest of the flight was smooth and uneventful. Finally, we landed at one of London's airports, Heathrow, exactly one hour after leaving Edinburgh. We had flown approximately three hundred and fifty miles. I was a long, long way from home! And I had arrived in England!

Chapter 4

MY NEW HOME

At Heathrow airport, I was collected by a curly-haired middle-aged lady dressed in a black jacket and wearing glasses. I had never seen anybody wearing glasses before, so when she peered into the carrier, I got rather scared and edged backwards as far into the carrier as I could. This lady, Mrs. Braithwaite, was the mother of my new mistress, Julia. Was it a kind sounding name? I couldn't tell.

Julia, I discovered later, loved cats, but was terribly allergic to them and suffered from asthma because of her allergy. Her nose and eyes would run uncontrollably whenever a cat was around. Julia thought that, by buying me, her allergy to cats would disappear, as I was furless. Maybe I would be the perfect cat for her; I liked this idea. I remembered what Mum told me about being special.

Mrs. Braithwaite placed me on the seat next to her on a coach going from the airport to her home town, Reading, about forty miles from London. Occasionally, she would check in on me during the journey, her glasses reflecting the lights of the coach. I tried to sleep under the blanket for most of the way, as I was tired and cold. I was also thirsty and hungry, for I had been travelling for so many hours without any food or water. So far, my new life was not going well. I was miserable.

Julia met us at the coach station. She was a pretty young woman with bouncy black curls. As Mrs. Braithwaite approached holding the carrier, Julia's face lit up. She took a look at me and was instantly smitten. Her dark eyes shone with delight, and I felt a little reassured. My new mistress was pleased with me. I began to purr, which impressed her further still.

"I can't believe that I am finally the proud owner of a *sphynx*, and he is so *friendly*," she rejoiced. Good bye forever, cat allergy!" Her husband Paul was looking on, a portly young man with small, almond-shaped eyes, blond hair and a black goatee beard. He smiled and patted her supportively on the shoulder.

Julia took me to her house, which was to become my new home. It was a modern, but rather small, house in a lovely and quiet area of the town, close to a small stream, which almost dried up in the summer. On the other side of a charming little stone bridge, there were green fields, but also some muddy areas. I must say, my new domain was rather small compared to the Macmillan's five-acre farm. I hoped there would at least be mice somewhere around there.

After a meal of my favourite cat biscuits and lots of fresh water - what a relief! – I explored my new home. It was certainly a bit of a climb-down from the very spacious Scottish farmhouse I had lived in for the first three months of my life! However, I was so worn out, that I soon laid down on one of the settees in the lounge and fell fast asleep.

The following morning, I awoke feeling refreshed. Only then did I realize where I was. No Mum, no Dad, no Coira. I looked out through the patio door. A pocket handkerchief of a garden, surrounded by a wooden fence, stared back at me.

"*That* is not big enough for me to run around!" I thought, crestfallen. But I soon found that Julia and Paul loved me to bits. They spent hours and hours playing with me. The Macmillans had donated the fishing rod toy for my new home, and I still enjoyed chasing the squeaky mouse that dangled from its end. But I did notice that Julia seemed to sneeze and cough an awful lot. She could always be seen clutching a tissue.

"Paul," I heard her say one day, "I don't think this can be a cold. I have had it for three weeks now. I think I must be allergic to Caligula!" My new master nodded in agreement. Poor Julia! She had thought that she was only allergic to cat fur. Little did she know that she was allergic to *all* cats, fur or no fur!

As I was making Julia so ill, it was soon decided that I should go and stay with Mr. and Mrs. Braithwaite, who lived a few miles away in South Reading. I could hardly believe it when I heard that I was going to have to move yet again. I had already lost my parents and my sister, whom I missed deeply. Now I was going to lose Julia and Paul, who adored me and spoiled me rotten with lots of delicious treats. Their house was rather small, but I had settled in and was starting to feel quite contented. My parents had not warned me that this would happen!

One day, before the move, I succeeded in sneaking out whilst the front door was left open. I headed straight for the stream. It was a place that reminded me of my home in Scotland. As I approached, two huge white birds came into view. They had large, dangerous-looking orange beaks. Frozen with fear, I stopped in my tracks. However, they seemed to be minding their own business and ignored me at first, so I stood there watching them. These must be the swans Dad had warned me about.

But after a while, one of them headed towards me. They had noticed me, and were not happy. "This is our patch," the bird sneered. Its partner loomed threateningly too. "Be off with you," the first swan continued, "we don't like your kind around here."

"But this is my territory," I pleaded, "it's my new home. I've come from Scotland." I remembered my mother's words: *purring will show others that you are polite and friendly.* Mustering all my effort, I emitted my best rumbling purr.

The swans did not seem to appreciate my efforts at purring. Nor did they really approve of what I had said. Before I had the time to realize what was happening, the second swan started to peck me on the back. It hurt. I ran as fast as I could over the field, away from the stream. Suddenly, however, I could no longer move my legs. I looked down and saw that I was stuck in sticky dark-brown mud. I started mewing loudly.

Fortunately, Paul had realized that I had disappeared and thought I might have headed for the stream and the fields. It was a typical thing for cats to do! When he heard my cries, he knew where to find me and took me home. I was so happy to be back home, safe and sound!

Unfortunately, I was so dirty and covered in mud, that I had to go straight into the bath. I'm afraid that I don't like being washed, so I cried in distress. Julia's sister, Maria, who was visiting that day and loved bathing me, was determined to get me clean. "We can't have you muddying up the furniture, Caligula!" she said jovially, as she scrubbed me with a rough flannel. Isn't water something that all cats are supposed to hate? To make matters more unpleasant, soap ran into my eyes, so I complained even more loudly. What a miserable day it had been!

Chapter 5

MY NEW PERMANENT HOME

One gusty September day, out came the plastic cat carrier again. When I saw it, I went to hide. The memories it brought back filled me with all the sadness and terror of my first move. I knew that Julia and Paul would bundle me inside and take me to another strange house. How right I was! After a short journey on the back seat of Mr. Braithwaite's car, I arrived at my new and final home.

This was a modern and detached house with four bedrooms, a large conservatory and a very large garden. Mr. Braithwaite opened the door to the hallway and released me straight away. Tall, with a large dark moustache, he reminded me of Mr. Macmillan. I had a good feeling about this place.

However, as I entered the lounge and climbed on the sofa, I stopped short, terrified. There was a strange black figure sitting on one of the chairs. When I looked more closely, I realized it was a cat covered in black fur, just like some of the cats in those pictures I had seen in my old Scottish home.

"Who are you?" he said to me "What are you doing? How dare you cross *my* territory? Speak, boy!"

"I am very sorry, Sir," I replied, trembling. "It's not my fault. Mr. Braithwaite told me that I'll be living here too." I attempted to purr, feebly.

"Right, then," the black cat replied, "but remember that *I* am the boss here and *you* must obey me, boy. I am Nero. *Sir* Nero to you!" I didn't dare contradict him, so I said nothing. "Well...at least you have some manners," he mumbled in addition and left the room. I wanted to tell my mother that her advice was proving to be very useful. But I also wanted to tell her that cats with fur were mean. I wished she was there.

Two other figures emerged at this point and sat on the two chairs: a female ginger tabby, and a black and white male. They were still much larger than me, especially with all that fur. I longed for the peace of my previous two homes. Now I was at the mercy of three bullies.

"Hello," said the ginger cat in a low, raspy voice, "I'm Mink. What's your name? Are you here to stay?"

"My...my name is Caligula," I replied, shaking.

"Well, welcome to our house, Caligula," Mink added. She was roughly the same age as my mother, and I secretly hoped that she might look after me. I was so relieved that Mink, at least, was quite nice to me.

The black and white cat said nothing at first, but just stared and stared. Finally he said,

"I'm Sabre. Are you really a cat? Where's your fur? What are all those wrinkles - you're old, right?"

"I'm only five months old, actually."

Sabre cut me off. "My gosh! Listen to your accent, it's really quite odd!"

"Yes, I'm from Scotland" I replied.

I was so glad that Sabre too had not been unkind and that Nero, *Sir* Nero, was the only one I really had to watch. I sighed with relief and told Sabre that I was a sphynx, and that I was born with wrinkles. He seemed to accept my answer and seemed unfazed by my presence in his home.

"Do *you* like tuna fish?" I asked Sabre finally. He didn't seem to hear; he had fallen fast asleep, right there, on the chair.

That night, I could not believe my luck when I discovered I had one of the upstairs bedrooms all to myself. I knew I would be safe from Nero's claws, as Mr. Braithwaite closed the door behind him when he left to go to bed. Also, later on, Mrs. Braithwaite bought me a comfortable bed in the shape of an igloo. It was so soft, that I dropped off to sleep the moment I laid in it.

I soon got into a routine at the Braithwaites' house! I love stretching out on the sofa in the conservatory when the sun comes through the glass. I am lucky to be able to enjoy a panoramic view of the garden through the windows. I can see and hear the birds in the trees, wishing that I could be out there trying to catch them.

I do a lot of that "clacking" Coira and I used to do when we saw birds. Mr. and Mrs. Braithwaite laugh at me whenever I clack. I don't know why they find it funny when they see my jaw trembling, but I am pleased that I can amuse them so easily.

Luckily for me, there is a fish tank in the conservatory, with a few goldfish swimming alluringly behind the glass. A cat-fish, called Rusty, lives there too. I love it when Rusty cleans the sides of the tank with his huge lips, when he is not hiding behind the aquatic plants. I wish the Braithwaites would forget to put the tank lid back one day, so that I could do a little fishing and hook him out of the water. What a delicious meal he would make!

Once or twice, I have seen an animal with a bushy tail running across the garden. I heard the Braithwaites saying it was a grey squirrel. I was glad I wasn't out there on its path; I was sure it would have bitten me. The other cats assured me that it was prey, but I didn't think I was quite big enough to copy them if they decided to chase an animal as large as that!

As time goes by, I am becoming very fond of Mr. Braithwaite. After all, he is in charge of my litter tray and keeps it fresh. I must admit, I do like a clean litter. All cats are clean animals and I am no exception. I might be a sphynx, but I am still a cat! I especially love jumping on Mr. Braithwaite's back, in a mad sort of way, from any surface. He says that I'm a bit like his parrot, and that he must be Long John Silver. I settle on his shoulders, purring happily. Sometimes I even nibble his neck. I follow him everywhere in the house and scratch any door that comes between him and me. Like any sphynx cat, I love human company!

Although I adore Mr. Braithwaite, I usually run away from Mrs. Braithwaite. She is always trying to do horrible things to me: she bathes me; she clips my claws; she sticks cotton buds in my ears to clean them. I hate all that! Nero, Mink and Sabre never have all those things done to them. How come I do?

As she feels sorry for me for being hairless, she is also always dressing me in jumpers and tee-shirts. She has even bought me a purple coat with a furry collar, for when she lets me in the garden on cold days. I feel really silly in that coat! The other three cats always laugh at me and say I look ridiculous. Even though I wish I had fur like theirs sometimes, I am proud to be who I am. I still remember the pride in my father's eyes when he told me how much money the Braithwaites had paid for me!

Sometimes, Mrs. Braithwaite insists on putting a little kilt on me because, she says, it is to remind me of my Scottish roots. She also insists on playing bagpipes music for me most days. This actually makes me feel quite sad, as it reminds me of my home in Scotland and the happy days I spent dozing on the red rug that had been my birthplace and listening to Mr. Macmillan's bagpipes.

Nero, Mink and Sabre are slowly learning to accept me and often let me play games with them. They even pretend to be my prey and allow me to grip their necks with my teeth. Actually, I think they are very patient with me, as I am so much younger than them. Nero, especially, likes me now, because we have something in common: we are both named after Roman emperors! He no longer insists I call him "Sir", but is happy with "Uncle Nero".

The only problem is that we all have to wait until he finishes with the food we are given before we can tuck in. We actually all have to line up: first Mink, then Sabre and finally me, last and least, it seems! I have discovered that all three cats enjoy tuna fish, especially Nero. I wish I could tell Mum.

I love it when Julia and Paul come to visit, as I became very fond of them over the few weeks I lived with them. I also adore Julia's sister, Maria, when she comes to stay at the weekend. She always spoils me with tasty titbits, lets me sleep under the duvet on her bed and gives me lots of warm cuddles, even though I make her sneeze too.

Well, on reflection, although I still long for my family and wish I could go back to Scotland to see them, I'm very happy with my life in Reading. I'm sure mine is a true case of living happily ever after! Perhaps one day, my new masters will take me back to Edinburgh to visit my parents. I think I could manage another trip on the plane if I knew I would be seeing them again. Above all, I would like to find out what happened to my sister, Coira. I hope she too has been sold to a nice family like mine!

Printed in Great Britain
by Amazon

32549696R00030